TEAM Cheer #4

THE
COMPETITION
FOR
Gaby

by Jen Jones

STONE ARCH BOOKS
a capstone imprint

Team Cheer is published by Stone Arch Books
A Capstone Imprint
151 Good Counsel Drive, P.O. Box 669
Mankato, Minnesota 56002
www.capstonepub.com

Library of Congress Cataloging-in-Publication Data
Jones, Jen.
  The competition for Gaby / by Jen Jones.
    p. cm. — (Team Cheer)
  Summary: Gaby Fuller is excited when she is invited to join an all-star dance team, but her friends on cheer team are starting to wonder about her ability to handle both.
    ISBN-13: 978-1-4342-2997-7 (library binding)
    ISBN-10: 1-4342-2997-1 (library binding)
  1. Cheerleading—Juvenile fiction. 2. Middle schools—Juvenile fiction. 3. Competition (Psychology)—Juvenile fiction. 4. Friendship—Juvenile fiction. 5. Interpersonal relations—Juvenile fiction. [1. Cheerleading—Fiction. 2. Middle schools—Fiction. 3. Schools—Fiction. 4. Competition (Psychology)—Fiction. 5. Choice—Fiction. 6. Friendship—Fiction. 7. Interpersonal relations—Fiction.]
  I. Title.
  PZ7.J720311Co 2011
  813.54—dc22   2011001999

Art Director: Kay Fraser
Designer: Emily Harris
Editor: Julie Gassman
Production Specialist: Michelle Biedscheid

Photo credits: Capstone Press: Karon Dubke, cover, 3; Geno Nicholas, 110
Artistic Elements: Shutterstock: belle, blue67design, Nebojsa I, notkoo

Printed in the United States of America in Stevens Point, Wisconsin.
032011   06111WZF11

SPIRIT!
Cheer!
Chant
SQUAD!
SPIRIT!
CHANT!
squad!
POM!
CHEER!
Yell!
SQUAD!
POM
FLY!
Cheer!
CHEER!
Yell!
CHEER!
Squad!
SPIRIT!
SQUAD!
JUMP!
FLY!
CHEER!
Cheer!
Cheer!
SQUAD!
JUMP!
CHEER!
Yell!
Cheer!
CHEER!
CHANT!
FLY!
CHANT!
SQUAD!

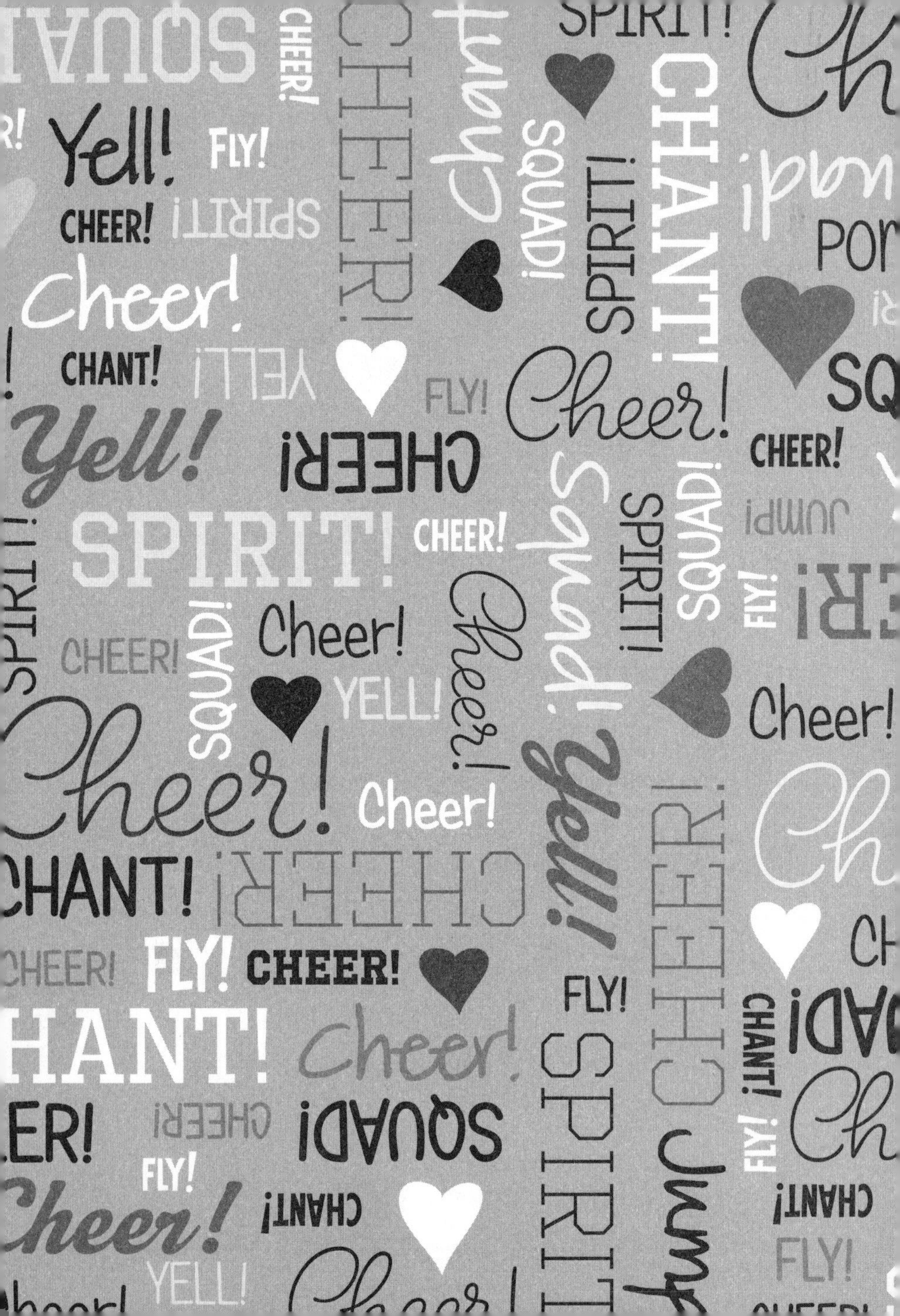

TEAM Cheer #4

THE COMPETITION FOR Gaby

by Jen Jones

Greenview Middle School Cheer Team Roster

NAME	CLASS
Britt Bolton	7th
Kate Ellis	7th
Gaby Fuller *	8th
Sheena Hays	8th
Faith Higgins	8th
Ella Jenkins	8th

Me! Squad co-captain and dancing queen!

Faith is my newest neighbor. We are all thankful that she moved into our lives and our squad.

Lissa is feisty and protective to the end, which is why it's great having her in your corner. But if she decides that she's mad at you, WATCH OUT!

Kacey Kosir   8th

Melissa "Lissa" Marks   8th

Trina Mathews   8th

Brooke Perrino *   8th

Mackenzie Potz   7th

Maddie Todd   7th

Coach: Bernadette Adkins
* denotes squad co-captains

My co-captain and the perfect complement to my somewhat carefree ways. Where I try to keep the girls going with my upbeat spunk, Brooke keeps us focused.

Cheer!
SQUAD!
CHEER!
Yell!
FLY!
JUMP!
CHEER!
SPIRIT!
POM!
CHEER!
Cheer!
FLY!
Cheer!
CHANT!
YELL!
SQUAD!
POM!
Jump!
Yell!
Yell!
CHEER!
SPIRIT!
CHEER
SPIRIT!
Cheer!
CHEER!
SQUAD!
SQUAD!
YELL!
Cheer!
SPIRIT!
CHEER!
Cheer!
CHANT!
CHEER!
CHANT!
SPIRIT!
CHEER!
FLY!
CHEER!
SQUAD!
CHANT!
Cheer!
CHEER!
CHEER!
SQUAD!
FLY!
Cheer!
CHANT!
YELL!

chapter 1

Being the only girl in a family full of guys might usually turn someone into a total tomboy. But not me. Nope, I was probably one of the girliest girls around!

In fact, my bestie Lissa was way more into boy stuff than I was. That's probably why whenever she came over my house, she ended up throwing footballs with the guys while I soaked up sun. Not that I didn't love hanging around with my four brothers, too. I'd just rather fish for finds at the mall than actually *go* fishing. Know what I mean? That was one of the reasons I couldn't get enough of my dance classes.

It was mostly girls at my studio, so I got to escape Planet Testosterone for a while. Plus, it allowed me to indulge my passion for fashion — whether it's '80s-inspired neon getups or a lime green tutu paired with striped tights. Thankfully our dance studio didn't have a dress code! Back when I was a little kid, I was always stuck wearing a boring bun, black leotard, and pink tights. (Can you tell I had been dancing forever?)

I was at the *barré* stretching when a girl I didn't recognize started warming up next to me. "Did I hear someone call you

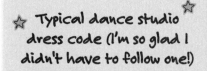

☆ Typical dance studio dress code (I'm so glad I didn't have to follow one!)

* No street clothing of any kind.

* Girls must wear long hair in a bun for ballet classes. It should be off the neck and out of the eyes for all other classes.

* Hair that does not reach the shoulders should be secured away from the face with a headband or barrettes.

* No jewelry, including watches.

* Ballet slippers should fit like a sock.

* Each class will be assigned specific leotards, tights, and slippers.

Gaby?" she asked, playing with her ponytail to turn it into a messy bun. She had some cool pink highlights under her jet black hair.

"That's me, the one and only," I replied, hitting a ballerina pose that made her giggle. "What's your name?"

"Marisa," she answered. She pointed to her head and did an exaggerated twirl in response. "It's my first day here. My dance team coach wants us to take classes in our off time, so I signed up for a package here."

"Oh, cool!" I answered. "So your school has a dance team?"

"Not exactly," said Marisa, putting her right foot on the barré and leaning over to touch it with her hand. "I'm on an all-star team."

I couldn't hide my confusion. "Aren't all-star teams for cheerleaders?" I asked her. I, of course, knew all about the competitive cheer teams that were independent from schools or sports teams. But dance all-star teams? Never heard of them.

"Well, yeah, there's a cheer team at my gym, too," said Marisa, shrugging like it was no big deal. "But all-star dance teams are becoming really popular. We go to competitions and train just like the cheerleaders."

"No way!" I said, squatting into a *plié*. It sounded so cool. "Believe it or not, I'm actually a cheerleader. Just for Greenview Middle School, not an all-star team. What gym do you go to?"

"It's called Energy Xtreme," said Marisa. "Have you ever heard of it?"

I hadn't. But before I could ask more, our teacher, Olivia, walked into the room. She clapped her hands to quiet everyone down. I gave Marisa an apologetic look and mouthed, "Let's talk later." I knew Olivia would flip out if we were whispering. It may have been a rock-and-roll ballet class, but it was still ballet!

"Okay, is everyone fully stretched?" asked Olivia. As we all nodded, she turned on some warm-up music. It was time to start across-the-floor exercises. "Everyone get in lines of three. We'll begin with *chaîné* turns," she instructed.

An old **Eurythmics*** song filled the room. I loved this class because it had the upbeat feel of a jazz or hip-hop class, but it allowed us to practice our ballet moves. To me, basic ballet was kind of a snoozefest, but I couldn't deny that knowing the fundamentals definitely made me a better all-around dancer — and cheerleader!

"Don't forget to spot, Gaby," called Olivia as I took my turn across the floor. I often got dizzy during turns. Spotting was an art in itself! I had a hard time keeping focused on a single spot while I made my spins.

Marisa took her turn a few lines after mine. I watched in awe. She was really, really good.

We continued going back and forth, practicing *jetés, pas de bourrés,* and some other moves. Marisa continued to

---

* The Eurythmics were popular way before I was born. But that doesn't mean their song "Sweet Dreams (Are Made of This)" isn't still amazing.

impress me with her elegant, powerful form. The class flew by. At the end, I noticed my friend Brooke watching through the observation window. We were supposed to grab some lunch, so I guess she'd come early to check out my class.

"Who's that?" asked Marisa, coming up behind me as I packed my dance bag.

"Oh, that's my friend Brooke," I said with a smile. "We're co-captains of our cheer squad. We're going to get some grub — this class always makes me so hungry! Our plan is to try this new vegan place a few doors down."

"I've been there — it's delish," said Marisa. She seemed so hip; I should have realized she'd already know about anything new and cool. "Are you vegetarian?"

I laughed. "Not even a *little* bit!" I said. "I'm obsessed with all kinds of food, especially candy and desserts. Brooke's the health nut, but I agreed to go because they supposedly have to-die-for cashew cheese fries and carob-chip smoothies. Do you wanna join us?"

Flora's Vegan Cafe

HOUSE SPECIALTIES

Veggie Scramble $6

Avocado and Cashew Cheese Sandwich $6

Tofu "Egg" Salad Sandwich $5

Cashew Cheese Fries $4

Mushroom & Bean Enchiladas $7

Smoothies (Carob-Chip, Strawberry, or Banana) $3.50

Fresh-squeezed Juices $2.50

Be sure to try one of our cupcakes
or cookies for dessert!

"Man, I *so* would, but I actually have practice," said Marisa, slinging her ballet shoes over her shoulder. "Hey, you should come check it out sometime. Lots of the girls have cheer backgrounds, and I bet our coach would love to meet you."

How fun would that be? I thought. "Mos def!" Then I saw Brooke, standing in the hallway with her arms crossed. She was pretty punctual, so she didn't like to wait around for anyone else. It was a miracle that she still hung out with me, since I'm not exactly the princess of punctuality.

"I gotta jet, but here's my email and phone number," I said, scribbling it down on some scrap paper. "Send me all the info."

She tucked the piece of paper in her hoodie pocket. "Perfect-o," she said. "Hope to see you soon!"

Gaby's info!
pomprincess98@address.com
555-4938

When I met up with Brooke, she was full of questions. "Who was that?" she asked as we went out the studio doors.

"I'm pretty sure Rainbow Brite called, and she wants her neon highlights back."

"Hey, they're cool!" I said in Marisa's defense, even though it *was* kind of funny. "She's actually a really good dancer. She's even on an all-star team. Besides, you're talking to the girl in a radioactive tutu."

"Good point," Brooke said, laughing. She gave my bright green tutu a little tug. "You two are birds of a style feather."

"Well, we might be birds of an all-star feather pretty soon," I told her. "She invited me to come check out a practice at her gym."

Brooke stopped in her tracks. "I hope that's a joke! Our plates are already fuller than a Vegas buffet," she said. "Coach Adkins would not be happy. You know she expects us to make the squad our first priority, especially as co-captains."

"Sloooow down, sista," I said. "No need to press the panic button! I'm just going to go see what it's all about — that's all."

"All right," said Brooke slowly. She didn't look convinced. I wasn't too worried about it, though. Brooke liked to do things by the book, but she'd come around when she saw that I could easily do both. And to me, that sounded like a pretty fun prospect! Gaby Fuller, all-star dancer . . . ready to shine!

Cheer!
CHEER!
Yell!
FLY!
JUMP!
CHEER!
Cheer!
FLY!
Cheer!
CHANT!
QUAD!
FLY!
POM!
Yell!
Yell!
SPIRIT!
CHEER.
Cheer!
CHEER!
SQUAD!
YELL!
CHEER!
Cheer!
Cheer!
CHANT!
CHANT!
CHEER!
FLY!
CHEER!
CHANT!
Cheer
CHEER!
FLY!
Cheer!
YELL!

Chapter 2

As painful as having four brothers can be sometimes, it also has its perks. Like when their cute friends come over! When I got home from lunch, my bro Tyson was kicking around a soccer ball in the yard with a mystery man. He definitely made me want to play **Nancy Drew***. Normally I would have made a beeline for the kitchen, but I decided to try to nab his attention instead.

~~~~~~~~

* I'm normally not a big reader, but a few years ago I discovered Nancy Drew. Can you believe the girl detective first appeared in 1930? Talk about star power.

"Yo, Ty!" I called, bounding across the lawn to snatch the ball. I held it behind my back to annoy him. "Way to bend it like **Beckham***— not!"

His friend laughed as Tyson ran toward me. "You gonna let your sister school you like that?" Oh my, he had a British accent. I made a mental note in my Nancy Drew files.

"Nope, I think she should go back on the sidelines where she

WAYS TO TELL IF HE IS FLIRTING!
· ♥ · ♠ · ♥ · ♠ · ♥ · ♠ · ♥ · ♠

• He tries to get your attention.

• His eyebrows raise a little bit while he is talking to you.

• He teases you.

• He looks you in the eye and holds your look.

• He goes out of his way to help you.

• He touches you when he's talking to you, even if it seems like an accident.

• He smiles the best smile ever!

belongs!" Tyson teased. He put me in a stronghold, trying to get the ball back, and we wrestled around for a little bit. He

* As my brother Tyson has told me repeatedly, on the soccer field, David Beckham is known for the way he scores by "bending" the direction of the ball so it shoots past defenders. Off the soccer field, Beckham is known for his fabulous wife, Posh Spice, and their cute kiddos!

finally succeeded, leaving me laughing and out of breath on the grass. His friend just watched with a sort of confused look on his face. Either he didn't have a sister, or things were a lot more proper at his house.

"Sidelines . . . oh yeah, you're a cheerleader, right?" he asked, taking the ball from Tyson and bouncing it with his knee.

"How did you know?" I asked, trying to smooth my hair. I probably looked like the mad scientist after my tumble with Tyson! "I didn't think high school guys ever gave the eighth-grade teams a second thought."

"Well, that's true, but the cheerleaders are a different story," he said, shooting me a sideways grin. Was he flirting? He was totally flirting! "Plus, we soccer types aren't lucky enough to get our own cheerleaders."

"Aww, poor things," I teased, swatting the ball away in midair. It landed at Tyson's feet. "We'll have to come watch one of your games sometime to make up for that."

"It's the least you can do," he joked. "I'm Matt, by the way."

"I'm Gaby," I told him. "I have to go inside and make a phone call, but I'll see you suckers later! Don't let any other girls school you in soccer while I'm gone."

Tyson just stood by, shaking his head. He probably wanted to get back to playing for reals.

"Fat chance," he said. "You wish you could school this!" He started doing some drills down the sidewalk. I just rolled my eyes.

"See ya later," said Matt. I walked into the house, trying to add a sassy strut for his benefit. I certainly hoped he meant it; I couldn't wait to see *him* again!

Suddenly I wished we cheered for soccer along with basketball and football. But even if we did, we wouldn't get to cheer for Matt and Ty anyway. They were in tenth grade, and I was just a lowly eighth grader.

When I got inside, my brothers Scott and Timmy tried to get me to play Wii, but I couldn't get to my room fast enough.

There were five kids in our family and only three bedrooms for all of us. But I was the only girl, so I got my own. (Another perk!) I logged on to my IM to see if any of my peeps were online. I was dying to tell them about the cute British boy!

Luckily, Faith was logged in. Along with Lissa and Brooke, she was one of my BFFs. I'd gotten to know her when her family moved in up the street from my house earlier this year, and she became fast friends with the three of us. I pressed the chat button and started typing furiously.

POMPRINCESS98: Girl, you need to come down here RIGHT NOW! Hottie alert in the front yard.

GOTTAHAVEFAITH: Oooh, I would, but I have Lissa here! We're looking through magazines to get inspired for the '80s routine.

I forgot about Matt for a minute and felt a pang of excitement. We had a competition coming up, and our '80s-themed routine was sure to be a contender! A "ding" sound snapped me out of it as a video chat request popped up from Faith, and I pressed the button to accept.

"Hey, Gabbers!" said Lissa, sticking her face into the frame over Faith's shoulder. "What do you think of my new look?" She batted her lashes, and I suddenly noticed she had bright blue eye shadow on.

"*Très** retro!" I exclaimed in approval. "Are you guys trying out ideas for stage makeup?"

"Yeah," answered Faith. "My mom even let us borrow some old albums for inspiration." She held up some classic LPs with Culture Club and Cyndi Lauper on the front.

"That's quite a soundtrack!" I said, giggling. "Girls really do just want to have fun." Faith and Lissa started doing some

---

*très = very in French, as in their '80s look was très awesome!

cheesy '80s moves and jumping around, but I got distracted when my phone started buzzing.

"BRB, *chiquitas* *," I said, running over to my bed to see who was calling. It was Marisa! I quickly picked up. "Hey, can you hold on a sec?" I asked, to which Marisa replied, "No prob."

I pressed "mute" on the phone and went back to my computer. "Girlies, I gotta jam — phone call," I told them. I didn't mention who it was because they didn't know her anyway.

"Oooh, is your crush calling already? You work quick," teased Lissa, doing a snake move back and forth.

"I wish," I said. I rolled my eyes. "Bye for now." I closed the window and un-muted the phone. "Hey, good to hear from you!"

"Word," replied Marisa evenly. She had that effortless cool that I so didn't have. I was always gushy and giggly. "I just

* chiquitas = girlfriends, as in I don't know what I would do without my chiquitas, and I don't want to find out.

wanted to let you know I talked to my coach and she really wants you to come to a practice. Could you come this week?"

"Um, I have to ask my parents, but it shouldn't be a prob," I answered. This was so exciting! "When is it?"

"We practice on Thursdays and Sundays," answered Marisa. "So if you could come Thursday, that would be stellar."

I did the mental math — we had cheerleading practice Mondays and Wednesdays, and games were usually on Saturdays. Wow, maybe this could actually work out! It'd be a little tight timewise, but I could totally make it work.

"Count me in," I answered enthusiastically. Energy Xtreme wasn't going to know what hit it!

Cheer!
SQUAD!
CHEER!
CHEER!
Yell!
FLY!
JUMP!
CHEER!
SPIRIT!
POM!
CHEER!
Cheer!
CHEER!
FLY!
Cheer!
CHANT!
YELL!
SQUAD!
POM!
Yell!
Jump!
Yell!
CHEER!
SPIRIT!
CHEER
SPIRIT!
Cheer!
CHEER!
SQUAD!
SQUAD!
YELL!
Cheer!
SPIRIT!
CHEER!
Cheer!
Cheer!
CHANT!
CHEER!
CHANT!
CHEER!
FLY!
CHEER!
SQUAD
SPIRIT!
CHANT!
Cheer!
CHEER!
CHEER!
SQUAD!
FLY!
Cheer!
CHANT!
YELL!

chapter 3

Before I could show Energy Xtreme my stuff, I had to get through my week. Mondays were always mega-busy. Not only was it the start of the school week, but I also had a tutoring session and cheer practice after school. Luckily, Brooke was my tutor, so that part wasn't too terrible!

English wasn't my strong suit, so we usually focused on that subject. Right now we were reviewing *Island of the Blue Dolphins**.

~~~~~~~

*Island of the Blue Dolphins is about this girl, Karana, who was stranded all by herself on an island. The crazy part is it's actually based on a true story!

Typically, I'd much rather pick up a copy of *Dance Spirit* magazine, but this book actually wasn't that bad.

Another reason I didn't mind tutoring was that we met at the Nook, a gathering area that Greenview Middle shared with the high school. It was a fun place to hang out, but even better, it could provide some prime Matt-spotting opportunities.

"Gabbers, you're looking everywhere but the page," scolded Brooke, calling me out. She could tell I wasn't all there. "What gives? I thought you were digging this book."

"I am. Karana's my girl," I joked, giving props to the main character. "But I'm kind of wishing Matt was my boy, so it's hard not to be on the lookout." I had debriefed her last night in a marathon phone call, so she already knew about my crush.

"Well, if you don't pass English, you're never going to make it to high school to be able to date him!" said Brooke. She was always straightforward, but I didn't mind her bluntness. Because we were such opposites, we complemented each other and made a good team — on the cheer squad and off.

"Point taken," I said. "How about this? I'll buckle down if you promise to watch one of Ty and Matt's soccer games with me soon."

"Deal," answered Brooke with a grin. We spent our remaining time wisely. When the clock signaled it was time for practice, I was happy for the break, but sad that no Matt encounter had occurred.

At practice, it quickly became clear there would be no time for daydreaming. We had a competition on the horizon! Coach Adkins relied on Brooke and me to keep everyone on track.

I still couldn't believe I had been elected co-captain. After all, I'm somewhat boy-crazy, often late, and have a slight tendency to goof off. But somehow I still made the cut! I guess Coach and the team saw something extra in me, and for that, I was extra grateful.

Brooke and I led a warm-up stretch, and everyone started to catch up on their weekends. Normally, Coach let us dish during this part, but today she wanted the floor.

"Girls, we need to focus!" she called, tapping her clipboard for emphasis. "Who has questions about competition?"

Sheena raised her hand, sitting up from her middle split stretch. "Is Trent coming today to help us?" Trent was a cheerleader at the local community college who'd choreographed our competition routine.

"No, Trent's job was to *teach* us the routine, and now it's *our* job to clean it up on our own," Coach Adkins said. "That's why we have to make the most of our time! Less than two weeks 'til we hit the floor."

"No Trent? No ***bueno****," said Lissa, who loved to use Spanish expressions. She had a little thing for Trent.

"You'll live," said Coach. "Anyone else?"

"Are we going to do a dress rehearsal?" asked Mackenzie, as we shifted into runner's stretch.

*bueno = good, as in Trent gave us a super bueno routine!

"Most likely," answered Coach. "We'll probably do a full run-through next Wednesday."

"Can we wear cool lace fingerless gloves like Madonna used to wear?" I asked. Our performance accessories were pretty much complete, but it'd be fun to add some funky finishing touches. Plus, one of the songs in the dance mix was "Material Girl," so it would highlight the theme.

Some of the girls nodded excitedly, but Brooke wasn't overly jazzed. "It'd be kind of hard to hold our poms with gloves on, don't you think?" she said, looking to Coach Adkins for agreement.

"Yeah, you're probably right," I said. But I still thought they'd be cool! Maybe I could talk her into it later.

> **OUR DANCE MASH UP!**
>
> "Hey Mickey" by Toni Basil
>
> "Material Girl" by Madonna
>
> "Let's Go" by The Cars
>
> "Girls Just Want to Have Fun" by Cyndi Lauper

We stretched a bit more, and then it was time to run the routine. The first notes of Toni Basil's "Hey Mickey"

played, and we yelled, "HEY VIKINGS!" over the "Hey Mickey" parts. Like many competition routines, this one started off with a fast-paced tumbling, stunting, and dance sequence, followed by a crowd participation cheer section, and ended with another brief music sequence.

One of the biggest parts that needed practice was the basket toss. A pretty tough stunt for an all-girls team to pull off, it required a flyer, three bases, and a spotter. Once the flyer loaded in, the bases' job was to launch her into an airborne toe touch. And guess who one of the lucky flyers was? *Moi!*

"Hanging in there, Gabbers?" asked Brooke after we'd run the routine several times. She knew I was new to basket tosses and might be running low on energy.

"Absolutely! I'm flying high!" I joked, flapping my arms like a nerd. It was true. I could have run the routine ten more times, but Coach Adkins cut us short. Practice was almost over, and we needed to have a closing powwow.

"Girls, the routine is really starting to take shape," said Coach Adkins. "Wednesday will be more of the same — just cleaning the routine and perfecting stunts and tumbling."

"I feel a first place comin' on!" said Lissa, making a number-one sign in the air. Kacey and Trina whooped in response. I hoped Lissa was right.

"If you girls keep performing like you did today, it's a real possibility!" said Coach A, earning more whoops from the group. She rarely gave praise unless it was deserved. "Now who can stay after school Thursday to hang spirit signs before the game this weekend?"

Everyone raised their hands. I started to do the same, then had a moment of panic. I couldn't — that was the same day as the Energy Xtreme visit. I slowly lowered my hand, trying to stay off Coach A's radar. Didn't work!

"Gaby, do you have a prior commitment?" she asked, frowning. She didn't take kindly to cheerleaders skipping out on group activities, especially me and Brooke.

"Yeah, I can't do it this week, Coach," I said, hoping to leave it at that. If I decided to join the all-star team, we'd have to have an in-depth chat about how to make it all work.

"Okay, but you still need to make at least fifteen signs," cautioned Brooke. She always wanted to be fair to everyone. "Give them to me before Thursday, and one of us will hang them for you."

"I'll put Picasso to shame!" I promised, adding it to my growing to-do list. Looked like I'd definitely need "xtreme" energy to be able to do it all!

SPIRIT!
Cheer! SQUAD! CHEER! CHEER!
CHEER! Yell! FLY!
JUMP! CHEER! CHEER! SPIRIT!
CHEER! Cheer!
FLY! CHANT! YELL! CHEER!
SQUAD! YELL! CHEER!
POM! Jump! SPIRIT! CHEER!
Yell! CHEER!
Jump! SPIRIT! SPIRIT! Cheer!
CHEE SPIRIT! YELL!
SQUAD! CHEER! SQUAD! Cheer!
CHEER! Cheer!
SPIRIT! Cheer! CHANT! Cheer!
CHANT!
CHEER! SPIRIT! CHEER! FLY! CHEER!
SQUAD CHANT! Cheer
Cheer! SPIRIT! CHEER! SQUAD!
CHEER! FLY!
SQUAD! SPIRIT! CHANT! YELL! Cheer

chapter 4

They say that good things come to those who wait, and by the time Thursday rolled around, I was crazy excited to try out Energy Xtreme.

Somehow I'd managed to keep my visit on the down low. Brooke hadn't really asked about it since Sunday, and none of the other girls really knew what was going on. It wasn't like I was trying to keep it a secret, really. It was more like, why rock the boat if you're not sure if you're on board yet?

My dad picked me up after school. He teaches biology at Greenview High, so he's pretty much on the same schedule as

I am! Even though it's only a 25-minute trek from GMS to the all-star gym, it seemed to take way longer than that. I was extra antsy and could barely contain my excitement.

"Dad, are we there yet? Are we there yet?" I joked in a little kid voice.

He laughed. "You're pretty into this whole idea, huh?" At my enthusiastic nod, he added, "I think that's great, honey. Just be careful not to overdo it. It seems like it'd be a lot to take on, with all your cheer practices and dance classes."

"Lots of girls do it and somehow manage," I told him, pulling a Kit Kat out of my bag to munch on.

"Okay, but are they managing to keep their grades up?" he asked, raising an eyebrow. I should have seen that one coming. "School comes first, you know."

"Oh, I know," I grumbled. I was sick of worrying about boring school stuff. Someday I could be a professional Hollywood or Broadway dancer, or maybe even a Dallas Cowboys cheerleader! Then I could make a living doing what

I love. I spent the rest of the trip daydreaming about just that, and before I knew it, we were pulling into the parking lot.

"Wow, pretty impressive," said my dad, surveying the sprawling brick building. A big banner by the entrance proclaimed, "Energy Xtreme Cheer & Dance Gym: Two-Time Worlds Finalists!" So their cheer team must be pretty elite — Worlds were the Super Bowl of all-star cheerleading. Now I was even more excited.

 ENERGY XTREME CHEER & DANCE GYM
Two-Time Worlds Finalists

When we got inside, I immediately dug the vibe. The walls were brightly painted, with inspirational quotes written on them in metallic marker. There was also a display case filled with trophies and team photos, and a TV sat in the corner playing team performances. At the reception desk sat a pretty girl I recognized from Greenview High, and she greeted my dad and me warmly.

"Hey, Mr. F!" she asked, recognizing my dad from school. "This must be your daughter."

I smiled. "Yep, that's me, Gaby Fuller. I'm here to practice with the junior all-star dance team today."

"Great! They work out over there," she said, pointing to a sign that read "Dancers' Studio."

"I'll go let the coach know you're here."

As she bounced off to tell the coach, I couldn't help but sneak a peek into the cheerleading area. It was huge! There was a large floor section covered with blue mats, along with a tumble track and a trampoline.

Girls — and guys — dressed in matching warm-up outfits were everywhere, practicing stunts and tumbling. For a brief second, I wished my own school squad had guys on it. I bet our basket tosses would really soar then! And more chances to meet new guys wouldn't *totally* suck, either.

I felt a tap on my shoulder. It was Marisa, dressed in an off-the-shoulder gray top with silver sequin trim and black leggings. I suddenly felt dorky in my sweats and striped tank top. "You made it," she said, smiling. "Here, I'll take you in."

I felt nervous butterflies all of a sudden. "Thanks," I said, turning to give my dad a hug. "Dad, see you in an hour or so?"

"Okay, I think I'm just going to set up shop in the waiting area," he said, holding up the book he'd brought along. "Break a leg! Oh wait, don't. That would probably make for a pretty short-lived cheer career." He could be pretty dorky himself sometimes.

Marisa and I headed into the dance studio, which had cool exposed brick walls and really nice hardwood floors. About twenty girls were inside already, warming up. A few looked up curiously when I walked in, but most just stayed in their little circles chatting.

It dawned on me that not all the dancers went to the same school. Maybe being on an all-star team was more cliquey than a regular school squad. Then again, a few girls on my own team, especially Ella and Kacey, could be pretty cliquey themselves.

A really petite blonde approached and offered her hand to introduce herself. "Hi, I'm Mandy. I oversee the junior dance team," she said. She was the coach? She didn't look much older than the girl at the reception desk. This was a far cry from stern Coach A, who was older than my mom!

"Hey, Mandy, this is Gaby, the dancer from Groove Studio I told you about," said Marisa.

"We're glad you're here, Gaby," Mandy said in welcome. "Today's actually a good day to visit because we'll be starting a new routine for a big flash mob at the mall next weekend. You can learn fresh along with everyone else and see how you feel about things afterward. And if things go well, maybe you'll be in the flash mob with us."

"Sounds perfect!" I said, clapping my hands in anticipation. I had always wanted to take part in a flash mob dance. How cool would it be to take a crowd by surprise with spontaneous dancing?! Marisa high-fived me and led me over to the cubbyholes to stash our dance bags.

The practice ended up being kind of like a mix of my cheer practices and dance classes. It started off with a warm-up and some across-the-floors, and then it was time to learn and rehearse the routine.

"Okay, so who has heard of **Thrill the World***?" asked Mandy, and a few girls raised their hands.

"Isn't it like one giant "Thriller" dance?" asked a girl with double French braids.

"You got it, Scarlett," answered Mandy. "It's a charity event where people all over the world do the Thriller dance at

---

* I really wanted to do Thrill the World last year, but there wasn't an event in my hometown. I was super excited to get the chance to participate in it, plus fulfill my wish to be in a flash mob dance at the same time. It seemed like this event was made for me!

the same time in hopes of breaking a world record. It happens every year around Halloween, and this year, we're going to take part!"

How cool! I'm a total Michael Jackson fan, and it'd be beyond fun to dance in a zombie costume. Everyone else seemed really pumped about the idea, too.

Mandy showed us a video so we could see the choreography, and then we started learning it step by step. It was fun to do music video-style dancing. Usually, I was doing crisp cheer choreography or disciplined ballet/jazz dancing at Groove Studio. And everyone really had a blast with it, letting out

As a dancer, it's hard to not love Michael Jackson!

MY FAVORITE MJ SONGS

Billie Jean

Beat It

P.Y.T. (Pretty Young Thing)

Bad

The Way You Make Me Feel

Man in the Mirror

We Are the World

Black or White

Heal the World

and of course . . . Thriller!

Michael Jackson-style squeals and moonwalking during the freestyle parts.

Afterward, Mandy met with me in the administrative office. "So Gaby, you were fantastic today! I can tell you've been dancing for a long time," she said. "Could you see yourself joining our team?"

"I totally could," I said. "I mean, obviously, I'd have to go over the costs and scheduling with my parents. Do you have any brochures or anything that I could take home?"

"Absolutely," Mandy told me, handing me some pamphlets. "Why don't you join us at the Halloween mall show next weekend, since you already know the routine? That will give you some time to think it over and see what it's like to perform with an all-star team."

"Perfect," I answered, beaming. "I'm sure it will be a ghoulishly good time!"

Dance
WITH
ENERGY XTREME!
CLASSES FOR EVERY LEVEL

1543 WEST BROADWAY
MORGAN TOWNSHIP
(555) 555-3487

Cheer!
CHEER!
Yell!
FLY!
JUMP!
CHEER!
Cheer!
Cheer!
CHANT!
SQUAD!
POM!
Yell!
Yell!
SPIRIT!
Cheer!
CHEER!
SQUAD!
YELL!
Cheer!
CHEER!
Cheer
CHANT!
CHANT!
CHEER!
FLY!
CHEER!
CHANT!
CHEER!
FLY!
Cheer!
YELL!

Chapter 5

When you're a cheerleader, life can be like that movie
*Groundhog Day**. Each week follows the same cycle: practices,
pep rallies, games — rinse and repeat. Plus that whole pesky
school thing! Right now, however, our squad was in limbo
between football and basketball seasons, so the weekends
felt somewhat strange without the usual routine in place.

But when the school bell sounded the end of the school
week, I was actually happy to have a free weekend ahead of
me. I was *so* ready for some R & R. I'd been totally on the go

* In Groundhog Day, Bill Murray plays this weatherman who is
forced to live the EXACT same day over and over. I started
to feel sorry for him!

lately! Plus, next weekend was going to be pure insanity now that Energy Xtreme was in the mix.

I kicked off my weekend of freedom with a snack with the girls. When I got to the Nook, Faith and Lissa had already snagged a table for us. They were drinking power protein smoothies, but I treated myself to some strawberry shortcake. It *was* the weekend, after all!

"TGIF," I said dramatically. "I've never been so happy to hear the bell!"

"That's what you said last Friday," said Faith, sipping her smoothie.

"And I meant it then, too," I joked. "It feels weird not having a game to cheer at. I was thinking I might hit up Matt's game Sunday. Anyone want to come on a stalking mission?"

Nook Specialties
(at least according to me!)

Turkey Club Sandwich

Two Cheese Quesadillas

Big BLTs

Cookie Dough Shake

Turtle Mochas

Strawberry Shortcake

Chocolate-chunk cookies

Parfaits!
(Everybody loves parfaits!)

48

"Ahh, the British invasion," joked Lissa. "I think I just might have to come along and see why you're so head over heels for this infamous British boy."

"Does he sound like **Robert Pattinson***?" asked Faith. "I bet he's dreamy."

But before I could answer, Brooke stormed in and plopped her books on the table. "Sorry I'm late!" she said, out of breath. "Mr. Givens called a last-minute student council meeting." Brooke was involved in about five million extracurriculars.

"Ain't no thang," I answered, slurping some whipped cream. "Did you guys take a vote to veto the mystery meat in the cafeteria? Even I can't stomach that stuff."

"Yeah, I don't see why the Nook can't be our cafeteria," said Lissa. "The stuff here is so much better."

"Not exactly," said Brooke, giggling. "We're going to be discussing ideas for School Spirit Week." She trailed off,

---

* Faith LOVES Robert Pattinson, but I'm more of a Taylor Lautner girl. I'm totally Team Jacob!

looking over my shoulder and lowering her voice. "Um, Gabs, don't freak out, but there's a really cute guy coming toward you."

OMG . . . Matt? I snuck a look out of the corner of my eye. Yep, it was him.

"Yo, Gabba Gabba," he said, making a cheesy joke about the Nickelodeon show of the same name. He was so funny! "Steal any soccer balls lately?"

"Ha, ha, quite the jokester you are," I said with a laugh, making urgent eye contact with Lissa. The look on her face told me she totally got what all the Matt hype was about.

"Oh, that's right, you've been too busy Thriller-ing it up," he teased me. "Ty told me about your big zombie debut."

My face turned red. I hadn't told the girls yet what was up with Energy Xtreme. He kept going, oblivious to my embarrassment. "So maybe I'll see you Sunday at the game?" he asked.

"Yeah, we're all going to come support you guys," I said, but my friends stayed silent. I was busted.

"Great, maybe you can wear your zombie makeup and scare the other team! See you then. Cheers," he said, bidding us goodbye in his cute accent.

Once he'd gone up to the counter to order his food, Brooke immediately jumped in. "Okay, what was that about?" She out of anyone probably had more of an idea what he meant, but was probably trying to give me the benefit of the doubt.

"Oh, nothing big," I said. "I'm thinking about joining this all-star dance team, and they invited me to do a Halloween-themed performance next weekend."

"Um, did you come down with amnesia or something?" said Brooke, folding her arms. "Our competition is next weekend!"

My heart sank. I'd been so excited when Mandy had invited me to the show that I hadn't put two and two together. Major fail on my part. "Chalk it up to Matt-induced temporary insanity," I joked, trying to lighten the mood. "I did forget, but I'm sure I can work something out. Obviously competition comes first!"

Always the peacemaker, Faith took pity on me and tried to be nice. "We know we can count on you, Gaby," she said. "So what was the practice like?"

I shot her a grateful glance. "The gym is totally tricked out," I said, excitement creeping back into my voice. "I wish we had the kind of equipment they have to practice on! And the coach was really awesome, too."

"So were you *ever* going to tell us?" asked Lissa, playing with the straw on her smoothie. She could be kind of feisty sometimes. "After all, you didn't know your future husband was going to spill the beans."

"Well, I'm still deciding whether I even want to be part of it," I answered honestly. "I didn't want you guys to think I was jumping ship."

"So are you saying you would quit cheerleading if you did join the dance team?" asked Brooke pointedly.

I was quick to defend myself. "Of course not! I'd do both! It's not like you don't have a zillion other obligations."

"You know what? I'm not thirsty anymore," said Brooke. I could tell she was getting upset. "I think I'm going to go."

Lissa stood up. "I'll join you," she said. "I've gotta go home and walk my dog." But I could tell she was kind of mad, too.

"All right," I said slowly. "But I'll see you guys Sunday for the soccer game?"

"Nah, I think Lissa and I will spend the day rehearsing for competition instead," said Brooke.

Brooke's extensive list of activities

- Cheerleader

- Student council

- Yearbook editor

- Tutor

- Choir

- Show Choir

- Band

- Library volunteer

- Volunteer dog walker

- Babysitter

- About 100 other things I can't think of right now

"I'd invite you, but it seems you're really busy these days doing other things." And she and Lissa headed off without another word.

I just looked at Faith, bewildered. I was trying to hold back tears. I hardly ever fought with my besties, and I hated that they thought I was being disloyal. I'd just have to prove them wrong . . . somehow.

SPIRIT!
Cheer!
SQUAD!
CHEER!
CHEER!
Yell!
FLY!
JUMP!
CHEER!
SPIRIT!
Cheer!
FLY!
Cheer!
SQUAD!
CHANT!
YELL!
FLY!
POM!
Yell!
CHEER!
Yell!
Jump!
SPIRIT!
SPIRIT!
CHEER!
CHEER!
Cheer!
CHEER!
SQUAD!
SQUAD!
YELL!
Cheer!
Cheer!
CHEER!
SPIRIT!
Cheer!
Cheer!
CHANT!
CHANT!
SPIRIT!
CHEER!
FLY!
CHEER!
CHANT!
Cheer!
CHEER!
CHEER!
SQUAD!
FLY!
Cheer!
CHANT!
YELL!

Chapter 6

On weekends, my phone usually rang nonstop, but I didn't hear from anyone. So by the time Sunday's dance class rolled around, Marisa's friendly face was a welcome sight.

"Hey, rockstar!" she greeted me as I sat down to start stretching. "How's life?"

"I've been better," I admitted, strapping on my ballet shoes. "My friends all think I'm **Benedict Arnold*** for coming to your gym."

*Benedict Arnold is one of the biggest traitors of all time, which is why my friends thought I was just like him. Way back during the Revolutionary War, he was supposed to be on our side, but he tried to secretly give this fort in New York to the British. Big-time traitor!

"What? That's totally ridic," said Marisa, scrunching her nose. "How immature."

I couldn't help but agree. "Yeah, I know," I said. "It's not like I couldn't do both. After all, I manage to balance my Groove Studio stuff with cheerleading just fine. I mean, my parents are totally on board as long as my grades don't drop. Why can't my friends be cool with it, too?"

"Why do they care so much?" said Marisa, leaning forward into a pike stretch and grabbing her toes.

"Well, we have this big competition next Saturday," I explained. "They don't want me to overdo it Friday night and then be too tired to be at my best."

"Tell them that you'll be even *more* ready to compete," said Marisa. "You'll be limber and still riding high from the night before."

"Truer words were never spoken," I said. "Plus, zombies don't need rest anyway!" I crossed my eyes and made a scary face, bending sideways into a new stretch.

Marisa laughed. I was glad my corny jokes weren't too uncool for her. I sat up and smiled. "Hey, what are you doing after this, anyway? I have to go to my brother's soccer game, and it'd be fun to have a partner in crime."

"I'll be **Thelma to your Louise***, for sure," said Marisa, grinning. "Let's do it!"

And we did, walking up to the playing fields together after class let out. There were plenty of familiar faces in the stands. Not only were my parents and my brother Damon there to support Ty, but I also saw lots of Ty's friends milling around. But there was only one face I really cared about seeing!

Marisa and I said hi to my family, and we took a seat a few rows down from them — after all, I didn't want to risk Damon hearing about my Matt crush. He'd never let me hear

---

* When Marisa mentioned <u>Thelma and Louise</u>, I couldn't help but think how much we clicked. After all, that just happens to be one of my favorite movies. Two sassy women on a runaway road trip . . . and one unforgettable ending. (And yes, it is rated R, and no, my parents don't let me watch R movies. But I did get to watch the edited version on TV!)

the end of it! I wasted no time scouring the field for that cute curly mop of hair, and spotted him in a blue-and-red jersey with the number 23 on it. As if sensing my eyes on him, he saw me and gave a little wave.

"Ooh, you're like his **Posh Spice***," joked Marisa, seeing the exchange. "Too bad you don't have her wardrobe budget!"

"I'd settle for wearing his jersey," I said. "Yum!"

More giggling and gossiping ensued, until I noticed a familiar duo approaching. It was Lissa and Brooke! I wasn't sure what to do.

They climbed the steps and stopped in front of us. "Hey, Gabs," said Lissa. "We thought maybe we'd been a little harsh on Friday, and we wanted to come by to say sorry."

~~~~~~~~~

* Things I love about Posh Spice:
1. She was a member of the Spice Girls. Yes, they are old school, but you can still jam to them.
2. Her fashion sense. She always looks good. And she always wears heels, which a little bizarre, but a lot fabulous.
3. Her hair. I mean . . . she got a haircut and it made national news. That is a true mark of luscious locks.

Brooke just stood there. I think she was sizing up Marisa, remembering that day at the dance studio.

"Thanks, that means a lot," I said, hoping that there wouldn't be tension between Marisa and the girls. "This is Marisa, my friend from dance class. Marisa, these are my besties Lissa and Brooke." I saw Marisa's eyes fill with recognition. She probably realized these were the girls I had mentioned earlier.

"Nice to meet you," she said, smiling. At least *one* of my friends had some manners.

The referee's whistle blew, signaling the start of the game, and Lissa and Brooke sat down to join us. It was Greenview High JV versus Dante Heights JV, and the game proved to be a pretty close one. It was exhausting just watching them run up and down the field!

"So, Marisa, where do you go to school?" asked Brooke. I was glad she was making an effort. It would have been pretty embarrassing if she didn't at least *try* to talk to Marissa.

"Oh, I go to Gilmore Academy," answered Marisa. Gilmore was a fancy private school in our area. I saw Lissa and Brooke exchange a look. They probably assumed she was a snob just because of where she went to school.

"That's . . . cool," said Lissa, her tone implying the opposite. "Are you on the cheer team or anything? Gaby mentioned you're a really good dancer."

"No, I don't have much time for things outside of dance. I'm pretty serious about it," replied Marisa. "I've been dancing pretty much since I was in diapers."

"No wonder you and Gaby get along so well," Lissa said. "She's our dancing queen! She choreographs a lot of our routines."

"Ooh, maybe we can use your talents at Energy," said Marisa, earning another look between Lissa and Brooke.

"There's enough to go around," I joked uncomfortably. Suddenly I was saved by a roar from the crowd. Goal! Made by Ty, no less! I let out a loud "woo!" and turned around to shake a celebratory fist at my family. When I looked back at the field, Matt and Ty high-fived down on the grass.

Marisa followed my stare and giggled. "Aww, bro-mance," she joked, and we both had a good laugh. Lissa and Brooke stayed quiet. I wondered if they thought we were making inside jokes. Couldn't we all just get along?

When halftime rolled around, Lissa and Brooke started packing their bags. "I think we're going to take off," said Brooke. "Gaby, see you at school tomorrow. Marisa, see you soon, I'm sure."

"Bye, guys," Lissa chimed in.

Marisa waved. "Peace out," she called as they made their way down the bleachers. She turned toward me. "Let's go get a snack!"

I was grateful that she didn't badmouth my friends. They certainly hadn't gone out of their way to befriend her. From my view, it was kind of cool having a new friend. We were such a tight-knit foursome that I spent most of my free time with Lissa, Brooke, and Faith. Maybe it was time to branch out a little bit.

"Now that sounds like a fabulous plan," I answered, smoothing my hair to primp for my prince. "Race you to the concession stand!" And we ran off in search of popcorn — and, of course, candy — giggling the whole way.

Cheer!
CHEER!
Yell!
FLY!
JUMP!
POM!
CHEER!
Cheer!
FLY!
Cheer!
CHANT!
SQUAD!
POM!
Yell!
Yell!
SPIRIT!
SPIRIT!
Cheer!
CHEER!
SQUAD!
SQUAD!
YELL!
Cheer!
CHEER!
Cheer!
CHANT!
CHANT!
CHEER!
FLY!
CHEER!
CHANT!
CHEER!
FLY!
Cheer!
Cheer!
YELL!

Chapter 7

I'd hoped the good vibes from my fun weekend would last me through the week, but the friend drama resurfaced once Monday rolled around. Brooke skipped our tutoring session, saying she had too much work of her own. And Tuesday, Lissa bailed on our scheduled choreography session, which was weird because she and I *always* did them together! She used the excuse that her mom couldn't drive her over, so she'd send Faith instead since she lived right down the street.

We set up shop in my backyard, and Faith plunked down on the grass to put on her Nikes. "I hope it's okay that I'm here instead of Lissa," she said. "I'm kind of a newbie to making up cheers and stuff."

"Of course! It's always good to get new ideas a-flowin'," I reassured her, even though I was still bummed Lissa blew me off. "Plus, we can get in some extra practice before tomorrow's dress rehearsal."

"That would be a-MAY-zing," sang Faith. She was always nervous about big performances. "Can we spend a little time working on my back handspring, too?"

Faith was starting to get the hang of it, but because she was so tall, tumbling was still awkward for her. Our goal was to get the whole squad capable of doing back handsprings before year's end. Faith didn't like being one of the weak links, so she always wanted to work on hers when we practiced by ourselves.

"Definitely," I said. "In fact, why don't we start with that?"

Faith stood up, and I spotted her a bunch of times. After a while, she was pretty wiped out and wanted to take a break.

"Okay, you sit down and relax," I told her. "I can show you the new chant I made up and get your feedback."

I launched into the chant, which started off with a diagonal motion and lunge:

NOTHING BUT NET, VIKINGS SCORE TWO MORE!

I repeated three times, getting louder each time. Finishing in **touchdown position***, I then added a high kick and spirit fingers for fun. I looked over at Faith expectantly. "Well?"

"Awesome, I love it!" said Faith. "You know, Gab, it would be a real loss for us if you ever left the squad. You're so freakin' creative."

*Touchdown position means my arms were held straight above my head, palms facing each other, hands in fists. When it was time for spirit fingers, I wiggled those fingers like crazy!

"Are you kidding me? Puh-leez. I'm stuck on this squad like Super Glue," I said. "I'm not going anywhere!"

"That's not what Brooke and Lissa think," said Faith quietly. "Of course, I know they're wrong."

I felt heat rush to my cheeks. I didn't deserve their doubts. I'd always put our team first and been totally dedicated! "One-hundred percent wrong," I told her with conviction. "Now let's work on this chant, and maybe we can even show them tomorrow at practice."

Faith smiled and sprang up again. "Spring Street sisters unite!" I felt a little better. At least Faith had, well, faith in me.

The next day, however, my pipe dream of winning over Lissa and Brooke with my rockin' chant didn't exactly come true. It started in the locker room when we were getting ready for dress rehearsal.

Brooke and Lissa gave me the cold shoulder, so I got dressed by Mackenzie and Trina instead. The tension was already stressing me out and practice hadn't even begun!

I really wished I had some Junior Mints. Nothing like a little chocolate to lift the spirits and calm the nerves.

"Hey, can you help me with my side ponytail?" I asked Mackenzie. As a nod to our '80s theme, we were wearing side ponytails with floppy gold lamé bows. We'd decided not to do fingerless gloves, but we did have layered socks on as another '80s throwback. Of course, we were also wearing our blue and red cheer uniforms. Glittery makeup would complete the look.

"No prob!" said Mackenzie, grabbing my ponytail holder. I saw Brooke watching from across the room. She was usually the one who played hairstylist for me. I just looked away.

Coach Adkins came in, beckoning us to get into the gym. "Okay, let's go, girls! We've got a lot to accomplish in the next two hours."

As we left the locker room, Ella caught up to me. I felt myself stiffen. She always had something snobby to say. "So, Gaby, is it true that you're quitting the squad?" she said. "That's the word on the streets."

"False as a *US Weekly* cover story," I said, hoping no one else heard her. The perked-up ears of Sheena and Maddie told me otherwise.

"Too bad. I'd happily take over as captain," said Ella, linking arms with Kacey and skipping ahead. "Feel free to reconsider!" Grr. She knew how to get under my skin.

I tried to collect myself as we kicked off practice. Drama or not, it was my job to co-lead with Brooke. We couldn't afford to let personal problems keep us from practicing properly. Everyone was pretty quiet as we got through the stretching part of practice. I wasn't sure whether it was nerves or the underlying tension.

"All right, let's run through the routine **full out***," I said once we were done. "Places, everybody!"

Lissa, Kate, Maddie, and Britt headed to the back of the formation. As our gymnasts, they would travel from back

---

*When you do a routine full out, you basically pretend it is the real deal. You do all the stunts, choreography, and cheers straight through as if you were performing for judges.

to front with a difficult tumbling pass. The remaining stunt partners stood in pairs across the center of the gym floor — Brooke and Mackenzie, me and Sheena, Ella and Kacey, and Trina and Faith.

Coach Adkins cued the music, and we obediently yelled "HEY VIKINGS!" as the music started. Sheena grabbed my waist and hoisted me into a high toe touch, and the other stunt pairs did the same in sync. Next, we loaded in for **chair sit*** stunts, and the tumblers passed through doing a **round-off, back handspring, back layout combo****.

~~~~~~~

* A chair stunt is sort of tricky to explain, but I'll try! A base holds the flyer under the flyer's bottom with one hand. Meanwhile, the flyer bends one knee, tucking her foot at the base's elbow. The flyer's other leg remains straight, with the base holding the flyer's ankle for support. Got that? Hope so!

** Our featured tumbling combo was sure to get the crowd excited. The tumblers do round-offs first. A round-off is a cartwheel that ends with the legs snapping together and feet landing at the same time. From there, the tumbler goes right into the back handspring, springing back onto her hands, then over onto her feet again. Then comes the layout — a back flip!

"Keep it going!" yelled Coach in encouragement. "Flawless so far."

We popped out of the chairs and rearranged our formation to make two groups of four, while the tumblers did choreography in front. The music switched to "Material Girl," and we loaded in for basket tosses. Faith, Mackenzie, and Sheena were my bases, while Ella, Kacey, and Trina were launching Brooke into the air.

"One, two, three, lift," instructed Faith in a whisper as I crouched down onto the bases' wrists. My hands were on Sheena and Mackenzie's shoulders, and Faith had her hands on my rear to push me into the air. We bounced as a unit and then I was airborne! I hit my toe touch in mid-air and then landed in their arms. Coach A gave the thumbs-up. Apparently, Brooke's stunt had gone well, too.

I popped out of the catch and we stood clean with hands by our sides. Then Trina clapped, and we all hit a jog to reach the new formation of staggered lines behind the dancers.

On the last note, we each hit Vogue-style poses to finish the opening sequence.

"Woo!" yelled Coach Adkins, trying to be a supportive audience of one.

"HIT IT!" yelled Brooke. That was our cue for the cheer portion.

BLUE AND RED

VIKINGS ARE THE BEST!

SHOUT IT LOUD, SHOUT IT PROUD

G-M-S

YELL WITH US!

G-M-S

ONCE MORE

G-M-S!

Then it was time for our second cheer, which ended with a large group stunt before the closing music sequence. All hands were on deck for the stunt, which featured me and Brooke on either side hitting **liberty heel stretches**, and linking arms with Ella, who was center in a **shoulder stand***.

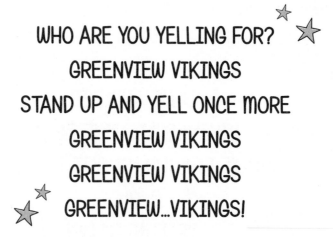

WHO ARE YOU YELLING FOR?
GREENVIEW VIKINGS
STAND UP AND YELL ONCE MORE
GREENVIEW VIKINGS
GREENVIEW VIKINGS
GREENVIEW...VIKINGS!

As we scurried to our places for the stunt, I accidentally bumped into Brooke. "Watch it!" she hissed, trying to get to her place in time. I tried to stay focused. I loaded in for my lib, but right after they raised me up, I lost my footing and

* Gotta love a liberty heel stretch! As the flyer, I stand with my feet in the hands of two base stunters. They hold me at their shoulders. Then I hold my unsupported leg by the foot smack dab in front of my head. (It pays to be flexible!)
** Ella's shoulder stand has her . . . you guessed it! Standing on a base's shoulders.

fell out of the stunt, taking Ella and Brooke with me since we were all connected. The bases managed to break our falls, but it still wasn't pretty.

"What was *that*?" said Brooke, standing up and rubbing her behind. "We've done this stunt, oh, about five hundred times, and never fallen out of it!"

I was so over it. "Oh, I don't know, maybe feeling like the people I need the most wouldn't be there to catch me if I did fall," I said, glaring at her.

"Girls!" said Coach Adkins, coming to stand between us. "This isn't helping anyone. If you've got something personal to discuss, do it outside of practice. Right now, we need to start from square one and get it right."

Brooke and I just stood there, staring each other down. We'd finally hit a boiling point, and the timing couldn't have been worse. A team divided usually didn't translate to a trophy. Would we manage to pull it together before Saturday? I was starting to wonder if this was where I really belonged after all.

Cheer!
SQUAD!
CHEER!
CHEER!
Yell!
FLY!
JUMP!
CHEER!
SPIRIT!
POM!
CHEER!
Cheer!
CHEER!
FLY!
SQUAD!
Cheer!
CHANT!
YELL!
POM!
Yell!
Jump!
Yell!
CHEER!
SPIRIT!
CHEER
SPIRIT!
Cheer!
CHEER!
SQUAD!
SQUAD!
YELL!
Cheer!
SPIRIT!
CHEER!
Cheer!
Cheer!
CHANT!
CHEER!
CHANT!
SPIRIT!
CHEER!
FLY!
CHEER!
SQUAD!
CHANT!
CHEER!
CHEER!
SQUAD!
Cheer!
FLY!
Cheer!
CHANT!
YELL!

chapter 8

Halloween has always been one of my favorite times of the year. After all, it involves dressing up, playing silly pranks, and eating lots of candy — what's not to love? But between the botched dress rehearsal and being on the outs with my BFFs, I was a lot less excited than usual as the big weekend approached. I could only hope that the "Thrill the World" event would be just what the mood doctor ordered!

My mom dropped me off at the mall around six on Friday night. We'd been instructed to enter through a secret doorway near the food court. After all, a flash mob wouldn't have much surprise effect if people saw the zombies before the music started! Heading down the long corridor, I could see Mandy, Marisa, and the others talking excitedly. When Marisa spotted me, she waved and jumped up and down. It felt nice to be on the receiving end of *positive* energy!

"Okay, X-women, we don't have much time, so listen up," said Mandy, trying to shush everyone. "I'm going to read off a list of restaurants, and we'll split into twos and threes. Each group will enter the food court from a different area, just like we practiced at the gym yesterday."

Mandy went through the list, and groups of dancers started to head off toward their destinations. When she read the name Sky's Candies, my hand shot up. Nothing like a little sweet tooth inspiration to start things off right! Marisa offered to pair with me, and off we went. Restaurant and store workers were in on the secret, so they were expecting us.

"So did you tell your friends to come watch tonight?" asked Marisa. "I figured they might come around after all."

> # If you find yourself at Sky's Candies, be sure to sample my faves!
>
> * **Sky's Popcorn Mix** . . . caramel, cheese, and butter all in one.
>
> * **Mega Jaw Breaker** . . . this can actually tame my sweet tooth!
>
> * **Super Sour Balls** . . . tangy and sweet? Hello!
>
> * **Homemade Toffee** . . . need I say more?

"How can I if they won't even talk to me?" I moaned.

"I'll take that as a no," said Marisa, shaking her head sym-
pathetically. "Well, try not to worry about them for right now.
This is Thriller night, baby! And what better place than the
mall for some retail therapy?"

I smiled but felt a tinge of sadness at the reminder of my
friends. They were probably all over at Brooke's listening to
'80s music and getting psyched for tomorrow. Meanwhile, I
was off doing my own thing with a bunch of dancers I barely
knew, except for Marisa. Based on the few practices I'd
attended, it seemed like everyone on Energy Xtreme already

had their set groups. But hopefully they'd gradually become close friends of mine, too.

I didn't have too much time to ponder, though, because the music was about to start in just a few short minutes! Marisa and I took our places hiding behind the counter at Sky's, much to the amusement of the people working there. "You guys want some candy corn?" asked one employee, taking pity on us as we crouched in our zombie costumes.

"*Yes!*" I answered, and she bent down to hand me a few pieces.

Suddenly a werewolf's howl echoed through the air, and I heard some shoppers start buzzing curiously as the "Thriller" music began. I couldn't see anything, but I knew some of the dancers were already entering the food court. People started to yell and cheer, and Marisa nudged me with a grin. "This is so cool!" she whispered. I couldn't help but agree, especially knowing that other flash mobs were doing this all over the world. Goin' global, baby!

Marisa and I were supposed to enter on the second verse, so when we heard "You hear the door slam, and realize there's nowhere left to run . . ." it was showtime! We stood up and left Sky's doing a Michael-like shoulder shrug and marching in sync. I saw a little girl point and giggle, and I tried not to break character and laugh myself. Other people just looked confused!

Once we got out into the food court, the energy was insane. Lots of dancers had already reached the center platform, and others were still coming in from all corners like Marisa and me. The routine was full of claps, shouts, and stomps, and the crowd was getting really into it as the song went on. By the time the famous "Thriller" dance part started, we'd all reached the stage. Then it was time to *really* get down!

As we did the choreography, I was surprised to see lots of people in the audience doing the moves, too. Apparently, I wasn't the only Michael Jackson superfan in the house!

At our dramatic finish, the food court burst into applause. Lots of shoppers came up to us and asked how they could get involved or do their own flash mob. One kid even asked me for an autograph!

Once all the commotion died down, we gathered at one of the food court tables to debrief and dish. I ordered a big Dr. Pepper and sat down by Marisa and another dancer, Charlotte. "Oh my gosh, that was hilarious," said Charlotte. "My makeup cracked, I was smiling so big!"

"I know. These flash mobs are a total rush," said Marisa. Energy Xtreme had done lots of them before, at places ranging from parks to school cafeterias. The whole idea was to catch people off-guard in a place that would never normally have a random dance performance. "What'd you think, Gaby?"

"It was utterly awesome," I agreed, mimicking one of the moves in my seat. And I meant it. The experience was everything I imagined it would be.

"I wonder what we'll do next," said Charlotte, munching on a sweet potato fry. "Maybe we'll find out at practice Sunday."

A lightbulb went on in my head. Not only was the competition tomorrow, but if I was going to keep doing Energy Xtreme, I'd have to go to practice Sunday. Suddenly a wave of complete exhaustion washed over me. "What's wrong?" asked Marisa, sensing the shift.

"I think everything just caught up with me," I said, trying to make light of it. "I'm totally pooped. But it's a good tired."

"Too tired to catch a movie?" asked Charlotte. "We were all going to walk over to the multiplex here in the mall and see what's playing."

"I think I'm dunzo," I said, checking my watch to see if it was time for my mom to pick me up.

"Suit yourself," Charlotte said, shrugging. I hoped she wasn't annoyed. At this rate, I wouldn't even be able to stay awake through the movie anyway! But one thing was for sure: if I was going to co-star on two different teams, I'd need to be on good terms with *all* the leading ladies in my life.

Cheer!
CHEER!
Yell!
FLY!
JUMP!
CHEER!
Cheer!
FLY!
SQUAD!
Cheer!
CHANT!
POM!
Yell!
Yell!
SPIRIT!
CHEER
Cheer!
CHEER!
SQUAD!
YELL!
Cheer!
CHEER!
Cheer!
CHANT!
CHANT!
CHEER!
FLY!
CHEER!
CHANT!
CHEER!
FLY!
Cheer!

Chapter 9

When my mom woke me up early Saturday morning, I literally felt like a zombie. My body ached all over, and my eyes were squinty and bloodshot. "Can I sleep a little longer?" I begged, burying my head in my pillow.

"You'll perk up once you eat breakfast. I figured you could use some fuel for your big day," said my mom, lowering a tray with an egg white omelet, some wheat toast, and a fruit bowl onto my nightstand. She'd even included a glass of chocolate milk — my fave!

"Aww, Mom, you're the bomb," I said. "Hey, that rhymes!"

"We've got to be at the convention center at 10:30, so make sure you're ready to go around 10," Mom cautioned me. "I know your makeup will take a while." I frowned, thinking about getting ready alone. Faith had tried to get me to meet them at Brooke's with her, but I'd refused.

My mom sensed my mood shift and put her hand on my knee. "Don't worry, this will all blow over," she told me. "Keep your chin up, Gabs."

"I'll try," I answered, wolfing down a spoonful of fruit.

I took a long, hot shower and felt a little better. Even without Mackenzie or Lissa's help, I managed to make a cute side ponytail. I even turned on some Madonna tunes to get me in the mood while I put my makeup on. An hour later, I was ready to hit the floor!

"Whoa, time machine," said Scott, looking up from his Wii game to see me coming down the stairs in my outfit.

"Lookin' good, Gabs," said Ty, who was lying on the couch reading a *Sports Illustrated*. "Good luck and all that. Even though it's not a real sport, I still hope you win." He was always teasing me about cheerleading not being a sport.

"Maybe you should take a cue from your loyal younger sister and come and see for yourself," I hinted.

"Fat chance, we've got a game, remember?" he said, laughing. "See ya!" I just rolled my eyes.

When my mom and I got to the convention center, there were cheerleaders milling about everywhere! About twelve teams from around the region were enrolled in our division, and the competition looked pretty stiff. Teams were running their choreography on the practice mats, and a few were hitting more difficult stunts than ours.

I looked around, trying to spot our signature blue and red. I couldn't help thinking that normally, one of my girls would be looking for *me*. Finally, I saw Coach Adkins waving in the distance. "Gotta go, Mom," I said.

"Knock 'em dead! Dad and I will come to watch later, of course," she said, handing me my poms.

I scurried over to the team, and most of the members had arrived already. Everyone looked great — and nervous. Coach A motioned Brooke and me to join her away from the group. "Girls, I really need you to step up today," she said sternly. "I want you both to address the squad when we do the pre-event huddle. As co-captains, you need to set a positive tone!"

"Yes, Coach," said Brooke, avoiding my eyes. I guess I couldn't expect an apology anytime soon.

Coach A nodded and walked over to help Kate fix the zipper on her skirt. Before I tried to fill the awkward silence, a competition official walked up to us, holding a bouquet of flowers. "Is this the Greenview Middle cheer squad?" he asked.

We nodded, and he handed them to me. "These are for you ladies. Special delivery!"

I tore open the card. We'd certainly never received flowers for competition before! It read:

Happy Halloween, Greenview girls!

I'm sure you'll spook the competition. Best of luck and bring it home!

Love and stuff,

Marisa

"Wow, that was . . . a really, really nice thing to do," said Brooke, reading over my shoulder. "Maybe we were too quick to judge her." She looked down, ashamed.

I was tempted to say, "Um, yeah!" but I held my tongue and managed a tiny smile. Brooke continued, "We really missed you this morning, Gabs. It wasn't the same getting ready without you."

I softened a little. I'd missed them, too. A lot. Even though I'd had a blast doing Energy Xtreme, life felt a little empty without my besties. I started to reply, but Lissa and Faith walked up. "Wow, flowers!" said Lissa, fingering the card. "I guess we were wrong about Marisa. It was really cool of her to send these."

"We definitely need all the good-luck charms we can get," I said, smiling for real this time. "My fall on Wednesday was not my finest moment."

"We were wrong about you too, Gabs," said Brooke quietly. "We should have known you'd never desert us."

"Yeah, I'm really sorry for the way I acted this week," chimed in Lissa. "Forgive me, *por favor**?"

"*Sí, sí, señorita***," I said, grinning. "Life would be way too boring without some Lissa spice in it!"

"Do I smell a lovefest?" asked Faith, smiling. "It's about time you guys mended the fence!"

Coach A poked her head into the group. "Girls, this isn't social hour! Get to stretching." But she was smiling, too.

Checking the event schedule, we found out we'd be going sixth. Everyone was pretty pumped, because middle

---

*por favor = please, as in por favor be my friend again

*sí, sí, señorita = yes, yes, girl, as in, sí, sí, señorita, of course I forgive you, my dear BFF

placement is pretty good for making a memorable impression on the judges. The cards were stacked in our favor — and as far as I was concerned, the pressure was on. Now that my friends believed in me again, I needed to deliver the goods today more than ever!

SPIRIT!
Cheer!
CHEER!
Yell!
FLY!
JUMP!
CHEER!
SPIRIT!
Cheer!
FLY!
Cheer!
CHANT!
SQUAD!
FLY!
POM!
Yell!
Yell!
SPIRIT!
CHEER
SPIRIT!
CHEER!
Cheer!
SQUAD!
YELL!
SQUAD!
Cheer!
CHEER!
Cheer!
CHANT!
CHANT!
CHEER!
FLY!
CHEER!
CHANT!
CHEER!
FLY!
Cheer!

Chapter 10

At a competition, the next best thing to performing was being on deck! And that's just what we were, waiting in the wings to take the floor. Some girls were pacing nervously, and others were jumping up and down or stretching. "Huddle up, everybody!" yelled Coach Adkins. "I just got the one-minute signal."

I shivered nervously, rubbing my hands together. I was trying to magically give myself more energy. We all got into a circle, linking arms and leaning in. "Okay, y'all, the moment of truth has arrived!" I said loudly, trying to be heard over the other team's music. I didn't want to let my fatigue show. "Our fans deserve nothing less than the best. Let's do Greenview's championship legacy proud." Our school was known for its successful sports teams.

"True that, Gabbers," said Brooke. "We can do this! Who's with me?" The other girls yelled and whooped, and we all put our hands in the middle. "On three, G-M-S!"

"ONE, TWO, THREE, G-M-S!" we screamed. "G-M-S IS THE BEST!"

"Shhhhh," warned a security guard standing by the stage entrance. We all giggled.

"Let's hear it for the Dunbar Middle Bobcats!" came a voice over the loudspeaker. "Next up, the Greenview Middle Viking cheer squad!"

It was time. We all ran out on stage, doing flips, kicks, and jumps — with giant smiles pasted on, naturally. Once I hit my starting place, I made a number-one sign, then quickly put my hands on my hips to wait for the music. I took a deep breath, trying to summon energy. "Hey Mickey!" the song began, and we were off! I could hear loud yells coming from our cheering section.

As we loaded in for the basket toss, my body felt heavier than usual. I forced a big grin as the bases launched me in the air, but it felt like I didn't fly that high — probably because I didn't push off forcefully. Still, the crowd seemed to respond positively. A big part of the score was crowd participation, so it was important to win them over!

We launched into the cheer part, and I longed for my megaphone. To my own ears, my voice sounded hoarse and raspy. "GREENVIEW . . . VIKINGS!" we concluded in unison. I breathed a deep sigh of relief that the yelling part was over.

The music came on again, signaling the final dance-tumbling-stunt sequence. It was set to a song by the old '80s group The Cars called "Let's Go," but all sped-up, of course. We stood in a triangle formation dancing, as Lissa and Kate crossed the floor in an X, doing an intricate tumbling pass.

Then the girls on the outside of the formation did a forward roll as the rest of us did back handsprings. As I landed mine, I fell forward a little onto my knee, but luckily, I was in back. I hoped the judges hadn't noticed!

"LET'S GO!" we yelled to the music with a clap, rearranging into the final stunt formation. We were arranged in three groups, with the flyers ready to hit **scorpions*** in the air. Once I was up, I kicked my leg back, reaching for my foot behind my head. I wobbled a little, but managed to stay up. Brooke and Ella hit theirs with ease — so Operation Scorpion was a success, much to my relief! It's not an easy stunt to pull off, especially when you're beat. I looked straight at the judges and added a wink for extra effect. We yelled, "VIKINGS!" and the routine was finished.

We dismounted and everyone started wilding out again and hugging. Offstage, Coach Adkins gave everyone big hugs

---

*Don't cha love how a scorpion looks? When a cheerleader gets her leg fully stretched behind her head, look out! It is fierce!

and told us we had done a great job. I tried to be enthusiastic, but I was suddenly flooded with emotion. It felt like all my energy had been zapped, and tears started to form in my eyes. We'd been working toward this for months, and I felt like I'd flubbed up. Sure, I'd squeaked by, but as captain, I'm supposed to lead, not lag behind.

Sitting in the stands, I tried to distract myself by watching the other teams closely. Pioneer Middle seemed like our biggest competition. Their choreography was really different, and they had made some really cool sign props. Plus, they could all do **standing back tucks*** . . . no easy feat! I could only hope I hadn't ruined everything for our own team's chances.

When it was time for awards, all the teams went onstage and stood in a half-circle. Lady Gaga played over the loud-speakers, and everyone started dancing around. For once in

*A standing back tuck is a back flip from the standing position, with the knees tucked in toward the body. A whole squad performing uniform flips is super impressive!

my life, I didn't feel like dancing, so I surveyed the crowd instead. There was Ty . . . and Matt! I couldn't believe it. They must have come after their game. So this was what Kirsten Dunst felt like in *Bring It On** when cute Jesse Bradford came to her competition! I gave them a little wave, hoping Matt hadn't seen my mistakes.

Faith nudged me. "Someone's smitten," she said. "Cute couple alert!"

"A girl can dream," I said, my mood brightening a bit.

We were interrupted by screeching feedback as the event MC tried to turn the microphone on. Everyone covered their ears. It sounded terrible! He tapped a few times and got it to work, then announced, "Okay, who's ready for the results?" Everyone screamed and starting stomping their feet. He held up the envelope. "I've got 'em right here!"

He began with the elementary school division, and then it was time for our part: the middle school division. "It was a

*Bring It On = Best cheer movie ever! Two fabulous squads battling for the top spot, plus a little romance on the side . . .

really tight competition this year, and everyone did a fantastic job," said the MC. I grabbed Brooke's hand, nervous.

"In third place, we have . . . Glenbrook Junior High! Way to go!" said the MC loudly. Their team started jumping up and down, and a few of the girls ran up to get the trophy.

After the arena quieted down again, the MC read the next prize. "Second place goes to a great team from . . . Greenview Middle School!"

Wait . . . that was us! Everyone started jumping up and down and screaming. But I stood frozen. I felt like we could have won if not for me. Brooke tried to get me to go pick up the trophy with her, but I pushed Lissa to go instead. As I'd suspected, Pioneer Middle ended up winning. Watching them get their warm-up jackets and huge trophy, I felt even worse.

Afterward, everyone was all abuzz, having fun and taking pictures. I could see Matt heading toward the stage and decided to try to collect myself in the wings. But I didn't get too far before Lissa, Brooke, and Faith stopped me.

"Why the long face, girl?" asked Lissa. "Hello, we got second! This puts us in a great position going into regionals."

"I know, but I feel like it's my fault we didn't get first," I said, the dam breaking. I tried to talk through my sniffles. "I had some bobbles, and I didn't bring it like I always do."

"Are you kidding me?" said Brooke. "Your fifty percent is most cheerleaders' one hundred percent! Don't be so hard on yourself. I didn't even know you messed up."

"It's not that," I said, wiping my eyes. "I just know that I'm run-down from trying to do five thousand things. When, really, the only thing I want to do is this." And as I said it, I realized I meant it.

Dance would always be a huge part of my life, but when it came to competition, cheer was my first love. I'd have to say *sayonara** to Energy Xtreme. I hoped Marisa would understand, and that we could still pal around at Groove Studio.

---

*sayonara = goodbye in Japanese . . . as in it has been great, but I just can't keep up with cheerleading and Energy Extreme, so, sayonara!

"Good, because we don't want to do it without you," said Faith, giving me a hug. "Now dry those eyes, because there's an Englishman just waiting for you to bat your eyelashes at him!"

My spirits rose a little. After all, Matt was here to see me, and that felt good. But mostly, I was relieved that all was right again with my friends and me. I didn't know whether Matt and I would end up dating, but there was one thing I knew for sure: I didn't ever want to lose my place in the Fab Four!

SPIRIT!
Cheer!
SQUAD!
CHEER!
JUMP!
CHEER!
Yell!
FLY!
CHEER!
SPIRIT!
CHEER!
CHEER!
QUAD!
Cheer!
FLY!
Cheer!
CHANT!
YELL!
CHEER!
Yell!
POM!
Yell!
CHEER!
FLY!
CHEER!
Jump!
SPIRIT!
SPIRIT!
Cheer!
CHEER
CHEER
Cheer!
SQUAD!
SQUAD!
SPIRIT!
YELL!
SQUAD!
Cheer!
CHEER!
Cheer!
Cheer!
CHANT!
CHEER!
FLY!
CHEER!
CHANT!
SQUAD
CHEER
SPIRIT!
CHANT!
Cheer!
Cheer!
SQUAD!
CHEER!
FLY!
Cheer!
CHANT!
YELL!
SQUAD!

Glossary

ADMINISTRATIVE (ad-MIN-uh-stray-tiv)—referring to management of an office, business, or school

AMNESIA (am-NEE-zhuh)—a partial or total loss of memory that can be temporary or permanent

ANTICIPATION (an-tiss-i-PAY-shun)—an expectation that something will happen

APOLOGETIC (uh-pol-uh-JEH-tik)—being sorry about something

CLIQUEY (KLIH-kee)—related to a small group of people who are friendly to each other and do not easily accept others into their group

DISCIPLINED (DISS-uh-plind)—focused and controlled

ELITE (i-LEET)—a group of people who have special advantages and privileges

ENTHUSIASTICALLY (en-thoo-zee-ASS-tik-lee)—done in a way that shows you are excited and interested

EXAGGERATED (eg-ZAJ-uh-rate-id)—made something seem bigger, better, or more important than it really is

INSANITY (in-SAN-i-tee)—extreme foolishness or unreasonableness

INTRICATE (IN-truh-kit)—detailed and complicated

OBLIGATIONS (ob-li-GAY-shuhnz)—things that are your duties to do

OBLIVIOUS (uh-BLIV-ee-uhs)—unmindful or unaware

SPONTANEOUS (spon-TAY-nee-uhss)—without previous thought or planning

Cheer!

Tell me the truth...

So I had a hard couple of weeks. Sure, I became fast friends with a great girl, but I also had MAJOR friction with Brooke and Lissa. Everything is cool now, but I can't help but wonder if I should have done things differently. What do you think?

- Was it wrong not to mention I was going to try out for the dance team? Do you think it would have gone over better if I had been up front with them?

- It really bothered me that Brooke was all worried about my schedule. Is it her business what I do or how busy I am?

- Did I give up on dance too easily? What would you have done in my situation?

Reading the forum pages of my favorite cheerleading magazines is one of my favorite things to do. Girls write their questions about fashion, parents, friends, and, of course, cheerleading! Help me write answers to these questions.

Squeezing it all in

posted by 2busy4all 1 day ago

I would really like to start babysitting more regularly, but I'm worried that with cheerleading, I might not have enough time for school and everything else. Any tips on managing my schedule?

I'm an outcast . . .

posted by sociallyawkward 4 days ago

I love to cheer, but it seems like all the girls on my squad are besties . . . except me! I feel so awkward around them at practice and riding to and from games and competition. How can I get to know them better?

If you're just entering the world of cheerleading, it doesn't hurt to read up on it a bit. (Let's face it. It sort of has its own language.) Even though I've been cheering forever, I still like to review some of my fave cheer books every once in a while. Like, before I choreograph a new dance, I like to review this section from a book called <u>Cheer Basics: Rules to Cheer By</u>.

EVERYBODY DANCE NOW

From peewee teams to the Laker Girls, cheer squads everywhere dazzle audiences with dance. Taught in "8-counts," routines can be up to three minutes long. Keep your dances from being duds with these hip tips.

PICK A CATCHY SOUNDTRACK TO CONNECT WITH THE CROWD

Oldies are always a fun bet, while hip-hop gets the crowd jamming with you. Avoid naughty lyrics or slow tempos.

PLAY DRESS-UP

Jazz up your routine by using pom-poms or props. Funky
accessories or costumes will also add flavor.

CREATE TRADITIONS

Pick a peppy tune or fight song to dance to at every game.
On the beat, yell, "Go [mascot]!"

MIX IT UP

For surefire crowd-pleasers, sprinkle stunts, tumbling, or
kick lines inside your routine.

STRIKE A POSE

Hold the ending pose for several seconds and let the effect
sink in.

* Excerpted from *Cheer Basics: Rules to Cheer By*, by Jen Jones, published by
Capstone Press in 2006

Meet the Author: Jen Jones

Author Jen Jones brings a true love of cheerleading to her series Team Cheer. Here's what she has to say about the series, cheerleading, and reading.

Q. What is your own cheer experience?

A. I absolutely love cheerleading! I cheered from fifth grade until senior year of high school, and I went on to cheer for a semi-pro football team in Chicago for several years. I've also coached numerous teams and write for a few cheerleading magazines.

Q. Did any of your family members cheer?

A. Some families are into football — mine is into cheerleading! My mom was a coach for close to 20 years, and my sister cheered throughout grade school and high school. My aunt and cousins were also cheerleaders.

Q. Which cheerleader from the series are you most like?

A. I would say I am probably a combination of Gaby and Brooke: Gaby for her outgoing, bubbly nature, and Brooke for her over-achieving, go-getter side. In certain situations, I wish I could channel some of Lissa's feisty fabulousness!

Q. What sort of goals did you have when writing the series?
A. My goals were to create relatable characters that girls couldn't help but like, and also give readers a realistic look at what life on a young competitive cheer squad is like. I want readers to finish the book wanting to be a member of the Greenview Girls!

Q. What kind of reader were you as a kid?
A. I loved to read and often brought home dozens of books when I went to the library. Whether at the dinner table or in bed, my nose was ALWAYS in a book. Some of my favorite authors were Judy Blume, Lois Duncan, Lois Lowry, Paula Danziger, and Christopher Pike.

Read all of the Team Cheer books

#1-Faith and the Camp Snob

#2-Brooke's Quest for Captain

#3-Lissa and the Fund-Raising Funk

THE FUN DOESN'T STOP HERE!

Discover more at www.capstonekids.com

☆ Videos & Contests
☆ Games & Puzzles
☆ Friends & Favorites
☆ Authors & Illustrators

Find cool websites and more books
like this one at www.facthound.com.
Just type in the Book ID: 9781434229977
and you're ready to go!